Tsuni

A short story

By

Joan Lightning

First Printing: 2024

ISBN < 9798877326460>

Published by P.J. Lightning
Bedfordshire, United Kingdom.

Contact- rykatu@hotmail.co.uk

Cover art by P.J. Lightning

Contents

Tsunimbus

1

Take a seat. Can I get you anything? Tea? Coffee? Something stronger? Oh, of course, you drove here. Coffee, it is then. Won't be a moment...

Here you are.

Well, let's get right to it. You aren't here for chitchat.

Yes, as agreed, you may record.

So, as they used to say in my youth, 'Are you sitting comfortably? Then we will begin.'

You want to hear me tell it in my own words. Listen well, then, because, as they also said in my youth, 'I will say this only once'...

To this day, I don't know what happened, not really. No one believed the survivors, but no one could deny that several dozen people vanished that night, and all that remained in the area was ruined houses, tonnes of water-worn beach pebbles, and puddles of water.

Saltwater, not fresh.

Also fish — extinct fish. Very extinct fish that have the scientific community in an uproar, but that's beside the point.

The pebbles, salt water, and fish are a particular puzzle because the place was a remote Scottish clachan — a tiny hamlet of rocks and sheep and little else but tourists – up in the Highlands, where the ocean was only just visible on the horizon miles away.

The authorities dismissed our memories as a mass hallucination brought on by shock. The world wants a rational explanation.

And Netflix wants to make a film. We'll be rich, at least. Hopefully, rich enough to move far away to another country.

I'd like to live the rest of my life somewhere where I can never see an ocean or a mountain again. Somewhere completely flat, with no strange legends, would be perfect. No clouds either — that would be even better. No clouds, no mountains, no oceans.

Do you know anywhere like that?

No. You just want to know what really happened. You and me both.

You won't believe it, my rational young friend, but this is what I remember.

Have you ever visited Scotland? Think rocks and shrubs and mountains and wind — lots of wind. We were coming down from a long day spent walking along hilltops with magnificent views of more hills and mountains. Ocean behind everything, sparkling in the sun.

It had been a perfect day, but as the afternoon progressed, the clouds began gathering and spreading.

So, we headed towards our holiday let, eager for hot food and drinks, and a relaxing evening in front of an old-fashioned log fire in the pub, listening to the forecast storm blowing outside.

We were walking pretty briskly at this point, hoping to reach the clachan before the rain hit. The wind was already bad enough. I didn't want to add 'soaked to the skin' to it.

We weren't far from it now. The track we were on would join a small valley, run along a tinkling stream for a bit, then swing off to the right to take us up into another valley. There, the clachan buildings were clustered on the slope — a mix of ancient bothies, and modern replicas built in the same style by a company that advertised it as a place to 'experience the true traditional life of Highland Scotland'.

True and traditional, if you overlooked the company employees in the shop and pub, and the electric lights and Wi-Fi. Although, one of those was generator-powered, and the other could be patchy — mountain valleys and good phone signals aren't generally a 'thing', after all.

Sorry? Who were we?

Just a group of friends. We'd known each other for years, since uni. We'd kept in touch and once a year we'd leave our families to their own devices for a week, to go on holiday together.

Always somewhere with mountains and views and paths. Always.

But never again. Not after that day.

2

"My God!" Jon, a little further down the track, stopped on the crest of a slight hill that obscured what was beyond. "Come and see this!" he yelled back to us.

Mark got there first and beckoned wildly, mouth agape. Colin, Dave, and I speeded up. A bit.

I mean, my legs were tired at this point. I wasn't going to jog just to find out it was only one of Jon's jokes.

I came around the shoulder of the hill into that little valley with the pretty brook. At least, that was what I expected to see, but the brook wasn't there; the brook had turned into a river — an actual thirty- or forty-foot-wide river.

And it didn't tinkle. It roared, bellowed, and growled as it raced through the valley and out of sight around a bend. Why I hadn't heard it until I saw it was a puzzle, but hardly the last puzzle of the day.

We stood watching the torrent for several minutes, partly because it was incredible and partly because the track we were following vanished under that flood. Well, we couldn't go that way, so we climbed over a dry-stone wall and picked our way along the slope. It wasn't difficult going, so long as you kept your eyes peeled for rocks and for cracks in the peat.

"Where's all that water coming from?" Dave said after a minute or two.

"Flash flood," Colin, always keen to display his knowledge, called back.

"I can see that," Dave replied, "But from where? Before you can have a flash flood like that, you need a buildup of water against an obstacle that gives way, or you need torrential rain for hours that collects into a torrent until it all drains away. There's not a lake in the area, and we've had three days of sunshine. Where's all that water come from?"

"It's cloudy ahead. Maybe it already started raining over there." Jon pointed. He was right: the cloud bank gathering above the distant mountains was thick and black. I could imagine torrential rain under it.

"Would it reach here so quickly?" I asked.

Colin shrugged. "Clearly, it has. So, clearly, it would."

We'd been shouting, to be heard over the noise of the river, but Colin's last words rang out clear and loud across sudden silence, and we all turned to look, and once more stood with our jaws open.

The water had gone.

The torrent had removed all the small plants and loose rocks, scouring the bottom of the valley to bare rock, where a small stream once again ambled along the path left by its larger and stronger cousin.

"Like I said. A flash flood, and now it's all gone past." Colin walked away. "Those clouds haven't gone away, though. Come on. I want to be inside before they reach us."

We followed.

"Can a flash flood end that abruptly?" Dave asked.

Jon repeated what he had said before, "Clearly, it has. So, clearly, it can. I've never seen one before, so I have nothing to compare it with. Have you?"

"No," Dave agreed.

The rest of us nodded; he had a valid point. The nearest thing to a flash flood that I'd ever seen until that day had been when the sewers were overwhelmed by torrential rain in the street where I lived. That flood had come on very quickly and disappeared even faster once the rain eased off. We went from no flood, to flood, and back to no flood, in the space of an hour. So maybe fast drainage was possible for this sort of flood, too.

"It gives some credence to that legend they told us when we arrived," Dave said after a minute's thought.

"What, the one about the shipwrecked Spanish galleon that appeared in the stream after a storm five hundred years ago? Dropped there by Satan himself?" Colin scoffed. "That's just intended for the punters. They probably made it up when they opened the business to tourists."

"No, it's old. I researched it before we came," Dave replied. "The story's been around for a few centuries. I even found a picture of a 19th century painting showing the last bits of it."

11

"I'm surprised. What about the myth of the monstrous fish that fell from the sky and fed the village inhabitants for a full week in the seventeenth century?"

"Also a genuine legend locally. No pictures of that, though."

"Well, there's nothing really very odd about a flash flood, even if we don't know where it came from. Shall we get on?" I suggested. "I'm hungry and I want a wee dram, as they say around here."

We kept going and soon reached the side valley leading up to the clachan. We saw immediately that the flood had come through there, too, also scouring the stream bed down to bare rock. The first drops of rain made us walk faster.

"Will the bridge be ok?" I asked.

"Should be," Colin replied confidently. "It's pretty solid, and well-fixed into the base rock, apart from the dry-stone walls. They'll be gone."

He was right. We soon reached the bridge. The water had removed everything loose for twenty feet on either side of it, but the bridge had lost only its side walls. The important bit was undamaged, with just a few puddles and a single flapping fish.

Mark picked it up and frowned. "It's a cod, I think." Then he wiped his hand, stuck his fingers in the puddle, and tasted it. "Salty."

"That settles it then," Colin said. "There must be a fish farm up there somewhere," he waved a hand vaguely upstream, "with artificial salt water, and maybe a dam gave way."

"A fish farm? Up in the Highlands? When the nearest ocean is in the opposite direction?" Dave snorted. "They build them where they can get sea water easily, not up here."

"So what's your explanation?" Colin said. "Go on. What else can it be? When you eliminate the impossible, what's left, however improbable, must be the truth."

"Now he's quoting Sherlock Holmes!" Mark rolled his eyes. "I don't care where it comes from; this is a large fish. I'm taking it. It'll make a good breakfast."

I was still looking up at the sky above the upstream area where Colin suggested the fish farm must be, but I wasn't looking for fish farms; the clouds had caught my eye.

"Look at that. Do you see it?" I pointed. To my fanciful gaze, the clouds were making a picture. Quite a pretty scene, actually. I pulled out my camera and took several photos.

"Funny how clouds can do that," Jon said. "That looks just like an ocean washing up against mountains in slow motion. It looks stormy there."

"The clouds aren't doing it; your brain is," Colin said. "It's called pareidolia. Pattern recognition. Our brains try to arrange things into recognisable shapes."

"We all know that, Colin," Dave said. "That one's particularly clear, though. Isn't it? The mountain almost looks real, and do you see that giant wave?"

I could see it: a swirl in the cloud, building, curving, growing, and looking exactly like a wave about to crash on a shore. I videoed it, zooming in and marvelling at the detail I could see. I stood there, not a care in the world, videoing a cloud, heedless of the drizzle; the scene was mesmerising.

The wave broke in slow motion over its spectral land, swamping it and sliding down the far side of the ghostly mountain as though it could reach the real earth.

Behind it, another cloud was already rolling forward, and another even larger behind. I remember thinking that I wouldn't want to be standing on that cloud shore watching a growing billowing tsunami.

I smiled at my fancy and turned off the camera. The others were already halfway to the clachan. I could see people standing around the nearer buildings. Tourists like us mostly, but also a couple of green-uniformed figures who worked for the holiday company. One of the latter, Sarah something-or-other, the site manager, seeing us approach, rushed across.

"Did you see Neil Crombie on the path anywhere?" she asked without preamble.

"No," I replied.

Funny how when asked something like that, we all had to look at each other and shake our heads as though checking that one of us hadn't spotted him and not mentioned it.

"He set off to walk to the lower viewpoint, half an hour ago. Said something about an owl he wanted to photograph."

"If he was on the path when that flood came down..." Dave said. "It was right across the track. We had to come along the side of the hill."

"Oh, my god!"

"We don't know," Mark said hurriedly. "He could have changed his mind and gone the other way."

"Or been washed to his death," Colin finished, heedless of the look of horror in the manager's eyes.

"We didn't see him," I said.

"Look, tell you what; I'll run down to the viewpoint and see if I can find him." Jon was already heading back along the path. "Try not to worry," he called back as he jogged away.

"Keep to the high ground," I shouted after him.

"Order some fish 'n' chips for me," he yelled back. "I'll be back before they're cooked." And off he ran.

"This rain's getting heavier."

"What are you going to do?"

"What caused the flood?"

"We need a search party."

The other holidaymakers crowded around, all talking at once.

Sarah visibly took control of herself, manager training coming to the fore. "All right, everyone, there's nothing we can do until Jon gets back. Let's get out of this rain. We don't know that anything's happened to Mr Crombie, but if it has, we'll call the police and get the search and rescue people out. Please just return to your bothies or the pub and if we need a search party, we'll let you know."

"The professionals usually prefer it if amateurs don't try to help," Colin said. "They don't want to end up searching for searchers as well."

"I hope he's ok." I stopped to look at the clouds again. "It's still there."

The second cloud wave was rising against that illusory mountain, tip curling over realistically. I shivered.

"Do you know what caused the flood, Sarah?" I asked the manager.

"I can't imagine. There's nothing uphill from here. No lakes or anything." She looked downslope. "I hope he's all right."

"I'm sure he is," Mark said. "I'll join you all in the pub in a few minutes. I want to stash this in the fridge for tomorrow." He lifted the fish.

"Ok."

I grabbed my laptop from my room and joined the others in the pub. Because of the weather, most of the menu was 'off'. All that was still 'on' was chips and ketchup and bread, so we developed something of a blitz camaraderie while we waited for the chef to peel and fry the potatoes. We ate crisps and salted peanuts, and discussed the strange flood, speculating about the probable demise of Neil, who'd been an amiable retired man with no family.

"Is!" I muttered to myself. "Is!"

"What? Dave looked at me.

I shrugged. "I was just thinking that Neil had been a nice, retired man. Then I realised I was using past tense. I hope he still is a nice, retired man."

"Yeah. Me too."

The Wi-Fi was a bit hit and miss, thanks to the weather, so I set my photos uploading and pushed the laptop and camera to one side while I drank coffee.

The chips had just appeared when Jon returned, panting. "I went all the way to the viewpoint," he told Sarah. "Nothing. I hate to say it, but if he went that way and was on the path when the water came down…"

"We'll have to call the pol—" Sarah's voice cut off as a rumbling noise began. "Not again!"

3

She ran out into the twilight, followed by all of us. I grabbed a handful of chips as I went and shoved them into my mouth. I had a feeling that the food would be cold before we got back here.

We couldn't see much; the sun wouldn't have set yet, not this far north in summer, but the storm clouds overhead threw the land into deep shadow. The rain had stopped, for which I was grateful; the noise, however, was deafening.

"That sounds like more than before. A lot more." Sarah said, slowing as she reached the corner of the path down to the stream. "Can anyone see anything? Let's not just run down there blind."

"Hang on." One of the staff, I never knew his name, ran back. He reappeared a minute later with a large, bright torch. Sarah took it and set off towards the stream, with all of us close behind.

We got halfway down the slope when Sarah stopped. The torch beam had touched foaming water. She swung the light from one side to the other, and then out over the water.

"It was nowhere near this far up last time," someone said.

"Where's the barn?" Sarah asked, pointing the torch in the direction of the large storage building where the company kept who-knew-what.

"Must be further downhill."

"Can't be. Or if it is, the water's even higher than I thought."

All we could see was water and rocks.

"Maybe it collapsed?"

"Are we safe here?" A woman's voice from the crowd. "Suppose it gets higher?"

And then the water drained out of sight. Just like before. All gone. We could hear it running down the valley, but after a few more seconds, quiet descended again.

Sarah walked forward, slowly, shining the torch from side to side. "There's the barn, or what's left of it," she said. "Jackie," she whirled around. "Take the landie and check the road bridge. I'm calling the police about Neil, and to report all this."

"Where's it coming from?"

"If that had come down when I was on the path..." That was Jon's voice.

The employee she'd addressed nodded and ran off. A few minutes later, the Land Rover roared into life and sped away up the rear track that led to the way back to the road, lights on full beam.

"Hey! The cloud mountain's still there."

I turned to look, and there it still was, just like earlier, just as real looking. Another cloud wave had just broken over the mountain and was streaming down the near side.

Heading for us?

"I've never heard of such a persistent cloud picture."

"When did you first see it?" I asked the woman who'd commented on it.

"Midafternoon."

"Does it look any different?" Colin asked.

"Not really. The waves are higher now."

"I'm surprised we can still see it, with all the rain clouds," I said.

It actually looked like it was in front of the clouds. Which was impossible, but that's how it looked.

"There's only two possible explanations." Colin shrugged. "Either it's a real mountain that just looked like a cloud, or there's some kind of local weather phenomenon that makes clouds in that area always look like that."

"If there is, I've never seen it in the five years I've worked here," Sarah said. "But it's not a real mountain either. It would be higher than Ben Nevis!"

She was staring at her phone. The light illuminated her face in blue, with eerie shadows thrown upwards. "Damn! Wi-Fi's gone out."

"Could that last surge have taken out the cable?" Dave asked. "It came a long way up the hill, and your cable isn't exactly well anchored going down the hill."

"It... may have," Sarah agreed. "It wouldn't be the first time we lost it to a storm. A bodge and fudge, five-mile wire, down a hill to the village, held together with a lot of electrical tape and prayer, versus falling trees, lightning, and occasional landslides. The wire rarely wins." She tapped at her phone and shook her head. "I've no signal at all. Not Wi-Fi or phone."

"I've got 5G. Nothing blocks that!" a man pulled out his mobile.

"The clouds are too dense, and the mountains are denser," Colin said.

He leaned closer to me to finish, "And some people are denser still." 5G man shook his phone and walked around with a look of disbelief on his phone-lit face.

Of course, most of the people present were now also pulling out their phones to check their own signals. There followed a chorus of 'Same here's and 'Nope's as everyone discovered that they too were adrift from the great web of modern civilization.

"The mountain's crumbling," Jon said. Like me and Colin, he hadn't bothered to check his phone.

He was right: the cloud mountain was slipping at last. Perhaps the wind had changed direction. It had certainly strengthened. As I watched, the mountain drifted sideways and the cloud waves behind it tumbled forward like a slow-motion tsunami, picking up speed. The movement opened a gap, revealing a bright moon and a single planet in the night sky.

"I don't like the look of that wave," Dave said. "Where's Mark?"

"I don't know. Haven't seen him since we all ran out here," I replied. I was shivering now. I couldn't take my eyes off the cloud racing towards us. I didn't want to listen to what the instinctive part of my brain was saying.

It wasn't making sense.

It couldn't be.

"He said something about packing his bag," Jon said.

"That must be Jupiter," Colin said. "Nothing else is bright enough to show so close to the moon."

I turned to stare at him. "Now? We get an astronomy lesson now?"

He grinned and turned his phone on deliberately to shine up from under his chin. "I thought I'd try to bring a little sanity back into the conversation. You're all acting like a cloud can turn into a flood and wash us away." He paused. "Well, technically, it can, by raining heavily and creating a flash flood, but not like that!" He pointed at the mass rolling through the sky, coming nearer.

"Neil Crombie may be dead. Your levity is beyond inappropriate," Dave said. "Especially as the second flood came higher up than the first, we don't know what's causing them, and we don't know if there may be a third on its way."

His pointed glance at the sky made clear that he believed that a third one *was* on its way.

"Right. I think we should—" Whatever Sarah thought, we never found out, because she stopped talking as we heard the rumble.

It wasn't like the earlier roar, and it wasn't like a rumble of thunder either. It wasn't loud, but it came at me from two directions at once: from my ears, and through the soles of my feet. The entire mountain was shaking.

4

"We had longer last time," Jon said.

"You aren't seriously suggesting there's a connection between…" Colin laughed, but it sounded forced. "Come on, be rational! It's just an earthquake."

Dave and I looked at each other.

The rumble got louder, the vibration stronger.

"Run! This way!"

Jon bolted towards the back of the clachan, where a gap in the wall led up into the hills.

I was on his heels with Dave close behind me. I don't know if Colin followed. I heard screams and panic from the others, but I didn't look back. I wanted to get to higher ground.

Earthquake or flood, I wasn't staying in the clachan to find out which. Fight or flight is a strong instinct, but you can't fight a flood. Mabe you can't outrun one either, but I did my best.

The moon threw just enough light to find the gate, and to pick out the path, stone wall to the right, rock-strewn hillside to the left. It wasn't enough to see the rocks on the path, but somehow, I kept my feet despite numerous trips and near-falls.

The rumble became a roar, the moonlight vanished, and I was scrambling on my hands and feet, no idea where the path was, no idea what was ahead of me, and not caring so long as it was higher than where I was.

Something caught me and I rolled. Above me, I saw... I don't know what I saw. A glowing eye? Were those teeth? Scales? Flippers? Was I already unconscious and not seeing anything at all in reality? That's what the doctors said. That's not what I remember. I saw it and it saw me.

And then...

I have a faint memory of more tumbling and pain before I woke in sunlight, lying in a pool of mud and dead fish, near the summit of a hill five miles from the clachan, soaking wet.

I was battered, bruised, and bleeding, my jacket in shreds, trousers torn, one shoe gone completely, and the other next to my foot but full of seaweed.

A helicopter was circling overhead. The BBC, I learned later. You can see me on their report; they were videoing the area while I woke up.

I could hear voices not far away: a woman gasping "Tom? Tom?", an infant wailing, and children calling "Daddy?"

I crawled a bit, but that meant having my face too close to the ground and the stench of things rotting. I forced myself onto my feet and headed for the voices. I barely noticed the rocks cutting my soles – a minor pain compared to everything else.

I recognised the woman when I saw her – another holidaymaker from the clachan, staying there with her husband and three children.

She clutched a baby to her with fierce protectiveness as she shouted her husband's name. The two older children – twin boys about eight years old – clung to her legs. All three whirled around with hope in their eyes when I lurched towards them. Hope which died when they saw who I wasn't.

Colin was lying near them, unconscious, but alive.

They didn't find Tom, or most of the others who had been swept away, including Mark and Dave.

At least, not then. You know about the bodies found on Ben Nevis, of course, and that Tom was washed ashore at Scarborough two weeks later, suffering from amnesia and frostbite, but alive.

The clachan itself was largely swept away. The walls of the oldest buildings remained, minus their roofs, but the newer structures – built to modern standards instead of the older ways – were gone. Only the foundations remained. A few other hamlets in the area suffered a similar fate.

And Sarah, of course. You know what happened to her. The conspiracy theorists want to make it all some huge government plot, but even they can't find a good way to explain how she turned up on the International Space Station a full two months later, soaking wet and still in the same clothes she was wearing that night.

Well, the lizard people theorists explain it with spaceships, I suppose, and some of the truly extreme nutters just say that it was all faked with AI. They're the other reason why I have so much security around this house. The death threats I've had are more insane than what happened.

And Neil Crombie...

Found in an excavation of a Roman cemetery in Cambridge, and identified because of the modern fillings in his teeth. The archaeologists swear that there were no signs of disturbance in the soil above him, and the C14 dating of his bones supports the Roman date. But that's impossible, right?

Jon, it turned out, escaped whatever it was, and was still on the mountain we had been running up. He refused to say what he saw. No money or pleas have changed his mind and now he's gone off grid.

I know you intend to try to find him. Good luck. I suggest you try Australia. If you succeed in tracking him down and persuading him to talk, I'd like to hear it. I told him about the eyes and teeth and he said that I was lucky that was all I saw, and that he wanted to get as far away from this area as he could. When I've got the money, I intend to do the same.

Which brings me to more mundane matters.

Now, you paid for the full package, didn't you? Let me check my records. Yes: five thousand pounds. So here are the prints of my photos from that day, and here's a USB with the raw files. Here's a copy of the video that the BBC took of me on the hill.

You recorded my story, but here's my written testimony, and this is permission to use it and my photos in your book within the restrictions we already discussed. If you need me to expand on anything, you have my email.

If you find an explanation, let me know. But it has to explain everything, not ignore the inconvenient parts, like Sarah in the ISS and Neil in Roman Cambridge. And it should also explain the other floods that were too sudden and too extreme and in places where they couldn't be. You know the ones I mean.

And that recent sighting of Nessie,

You laugh, I see. But, of course, that last bit was a joke.

Just a joke.

I'll show you out. I want to check the sky. I always look several times a day, just in case.

Oh!

Do you see that? Those clouds? You do?

The mountains and coastline look so realistic, and it looks like the wind's getting up over there.

I think I may go away for a few days. I suggest you do as well.

In fact, I'm leaving right now.

Acknowledgements

Thanks go to my alpha reader/editor TS Arthur. Any mistakes you may spot, are entirely my fault.

Thanks are also due to the members of several Facebook groups, including but not limited to The Writers Forum, Fantasy Writers Critique and Support Group, and Clean Indie Reads. The cover and blurb are a thousand times better than they would have been without the members of these groups.

About the author

I'm a sixty-something Christian, archaeologist, martial arts practitioner, and amateur photographer. I was introduced to science fiction and fantasy at a young age by my best friend's dad, who had boxes and boxes of science fiction books dating to the 50s, 60s, and 70s.

In those boxes, I met Isaac Asimov, Frank Herbert, Anne McCaffrey, Zenna Henderson, and many more, and I learned to love the smell of a printed volume.

I started telling stories to my nephews to while away long car journeys, and one day decided to accept a challenge to write a shot story about a race of people called the Tyreans.

Fourteen years later, here I am, still telling tales set in that world, but also branching out to try some other genres, like the book in your hand.

Books:

Epic Fantasy.
Falling Shadows. Guardians of Reyth volume 1
The Angate Conspiracy. Guardians of Reyth volume 2
To Collar the Cat. Guardians of Reyth volume 3
Journey to Bein. Guardians of Reyth volume 4
Cost of Duty. Guardians of Reyth volume 5
Path of Shadows. Guardians of Reyth volume 6
Storm's End. Guardians of Reyth volume 7

The Flowers of Ishfalen. Recitors of Kandar volume 1
Dreadthorns in Aryanta. Recitors of Kandar volume 2
The Crystals of Erimess. Recitors of Kandar volume 3 (due Dec 2024.)

Shorts stories and novellas set on Reyth.
Origins
Norin
Shadow of the Past.
Sorcerer's Duty.
Mistaken Strength.

Christian Supernatural
Chosen?

Non-fiction. WW2.
With all my Love

Printed in Great Britain
by Amazon

37173840R00020